THIS BOOK BELONGS TO

Anna Mewkill
If found please
~~& call:~~ 978-526-4744

PUFFIN BOOKS

Published by the Penguin Group
Melbourne • London • New York • Toronto • Dublin
New Delhi • Auckland • Johannesburg
Penguin Books Ltd, Registered Offices: 80 Strand, London WC2R 0RL, England
Published by Penguin Group (Australia), 2011
10 9 8 7 6 5 4 3

Typeset in Bembo by Post Pre-press Group, Brisbane, Queensland
Printed and bound in Australia by McPherson's Printing Group, Maryborough, Victoria
National Library of Australia Cataloguing-in-Publication data available.

ISBN 978 0 14 330536 1

Poster on page 104 reprinted with kind permission from the
Parliament Art House Collection

puffin.com.au
ouraustraliangirl.com.au

Charms on the front cover reprinted with kind permission from A&E Metal Merchants.
www.aemetals.com.au

OUR
AUSTRALIAN
GIRL

Meet Rose

It's 1900 and Rose lives with her family in a big house in Melbourne. She wants to play cricket, climb trees and be an adventurer! But Rose's mother has other ideas, and only wants Rose to be a proper lady, wear frilly dresses and learn how to sew. Then Rose's favourite young aunt, Alice, comes to town, and everything changes. Will Rose's mother let Aunt Alice stay? And will Rose ever get to do the things she really loves?

Meet Rose and join her adventure in the first of four stories about a Federation girl who's determined to do things her way!

Puffin Books

 *For Brian*

OUR AUSTRALIAN GIRL

Meet Rose

Sherryl Clark

With illustrations by Lucia Masciullo

Puffin Books

AUSTRALIA

1900

Western Australia

South

ROSE'S STORY

Rose wants to ride a bicycle and play cricket and
travel the world. Share in Rose's remarkable
adventures as you read this story of a determined
Australian girl.

N

W · E

S

10

20

30

40

50

60

70

80

150 · 160 · 170 · 180 · 190

Queensland

Australia

New South Wales

Victoria

Tasmania

♥ Where this story takes place

0 I II III IV V VI VII VIII IX X

1
Birthday Girl

WHEN Rose heard the soft tap on her bedroom door, she joined her brother, Edward, in the dark corridor. Apart from the distant sound of Father snoring and a few birds in the trees outside, all was quiet. Edward was carrying his cricket bat and ball, and he grinned at her, his teeth white in the gloom.

They crept down the wide staircase, past the tall stained-glass windows above the landing and out the front door, closing it behind them with a click. Dawn painted the sky a pale pink and dew coated the lawns.

'Happy birthday,' Edward whispered. 'You want to bowl first?'

'Of course!' Rose said.

They avoided the crunchy gravel on the driveway and ran around to the back of their huge house, past the stables and down to the farthest corner, where Edward had set up his wickets. He'd promised to play cricket with Rose on her birthday, and this was the only chance they'd have before Mother would wake up and come looking for her.

Edward poked at the grass with his bat. 'It must've rained last night.'

Rose laughed as she warmed up her bowling arm, swinging it around and up. 'Not making excuses already, are you Ed?'

'Just bowl,' Edward said.

The ball floated through the air, bounced, and Edward swung at it, clipping it on the edge. It disappeared into the bushes behind him. Rose grinned. She loved bowling her tricky spinners, and even though Edward was older and taller than her, she'd soon get him out and then she could have a turn.

They'd had one bat each when a shrill voice called, 'Rose! Are you out here? Rose?' It was her governess, Miss Parson.

Rose wanted to run and hide in the bushes, but that would only get her into more trouble. She handed the cricket ball to Edward. 'I'd better go before she busts a boiler.'

Miss Parson was waiting near the kitchen door, a scowl on her narrow, pale face. 'What were you doing out so early?' she asked.

'Walking,' Rose said. She wasn't in the habit of telling fibs, but surely a small lie to Miss Parson didn't count. 'It's a lovely morning.'

'Hmph.' Miss Parson followed her inside and up the stairs. 'Your mother expects you down for breakfast in five minutes, and your boots are dirty.'

'Yes, Miss Parson.'

In her bedroom, Rose poured cold water from the flowered jug into the bowl and washed her hands and face, shivering at how icy it was. She used the hand towel to clean her boots, and brushed her dark, unruly hair. There. Surely Mother wouldn't scold her on her birthday? Miss Parson came in without knocking and Rose glared.

'Come on, hurry up,' said Miss Parson. 'And pull up your stockings. They're a disgrace.'

Rose yanked them up and heard an awful ripping sound. She looked down at the large hole she'd just made. 'Oops.'

Miss Parson huffed loudly. 'Too much haste, not enough care – as usual.'

'But Sally will mend it in an instant!'

'And what will you learn from that?' Miss Parson asked. 'No, you can sew it yourself today instead of working on your doily stitching. Or I can tell your mother and let her give you a suitable punishment.'

Sewing was already like a punishment for
Rose. She'd much rather be outside, climbing
trees or digging in the garden. 'I'll do it myself,'
she said. Miss Parson followed her down the
stairs and went off to the kitchen, while Rose
continued on to the breakfast room, where
she spotted a small pile of gifts by her plate.
There was no way she'd let Miss Parson ruin
her birthday, especially with all those surprises
waiting!

The rest of her family was already seated,
her father reading the newspaper, *The Argus*.

'Happy birthday, Rose!' everyone chorused.

'Open your presents,' Martha said. Rose's
older sister always gave her something small
and special.

Mother tapped her plate with a spoon. 'Eat
your breakfast first, Rose. The gifts can wait.'

'But ...' Rose shrugged. It was useless to
argue with Mother. Rose took her plate to the
sideboard impatiently, ready to choose some

eggs and bacon, but there were only kippers and porridge. She hated kippers – even more than sardines – Mother knew that! Tears stung her eyes, but she bit her lip, determined not to cry. She helped herself to porridge instead, and stirred in four big spoonfuls of sugar and some preserved peaches before Mother noticed.

Rose ate quickly and was finally allowed to open her presents. She decided to leave Martha's until last. Mother and Father gave her gloves and a parasol. Edward's was shaped like a book, which was what she really wanted, but it turned out to be a box of glâcé cherries. She glanced at him and he mouthed, 'Sorry.' That meant Mother had bought the cherries and put his name on the card. Rose put all her hopes into the last gift, the smallest one.

She pulled the paper off and opened the little box. Nestled inside was a tiny gold oval locket engraved with birds. 'It's beautiful,' Rose said.

'Thank you.' She jumped up and gave Martha a hug and a kiss, breathing in her perfume.

Martha laughed and smoothed Rose's hair with her soft hands. She was always dressed so perfectly, her pretty face framed by her swept-up dark hair.

'What about everyone else?' Mother said, tilting her head so Rose could kiss her cheek.

'Eleven now, eh, Rose?' Father said. 'You'll be married before we know it.' He winked and Rose laughed. Father already knew that Rose planned to become an explorer and travel the world instead of getting married.

When Rose kissed Edward, he whispered, 'Here's your real present,' and shoved his cricket ball into her hand. Luckily, Mother was already on her way out of the breakfast room and didn't see.

'Holy smoke!' Rose said. 'Are you sure?'

Edward nodded. 'Have a nice birthday. Are you still going to the park?'

'I hope so.' Mother hadn't actually promised when Rose had asked, but she hadn't said no either.

Until then, though, it was lessons as usual with Miss Parson, which meant an hour of reading from a storybook Rose nearly knew by heart and then mending her ripped stocking. She made such a mess of the stitches that Miss Parson had to give it to Sally, the housemaid, after all. Rose desperately wished Miss Parson could teach more than needlework and French verbs. Rose wanted to learn geography and history, like Edward, and study insects and fossils. However, she could just imagine Miss Parson turning her nose up at a dinosaur bone!

At lunch, Mother said, 'Now, I expect you to be ready by three o'clock.'

'Isn't that a little late for the park?' Rose said.

'We're not going out,' Mother said. 'Your grandmother and Uncle Charles and Aunt Philippa are coming for afternoon tea.'

'But what about the park?'

'Don't be silly, Rose,' Mother said. 'They are visiting for your birthday. You should be grateful. No doubt they will bring gifts.'

Hot anger rushed through Rose and she clenched her hands. 'I don't care! I've been looking forward to the park all day!'

'Fetch Miss Parson,' Mother snapped to Sally.

Rose waited in silence, face burning, as Miss Parson rushed in. 'Yes, Madam,' she said.

'Please ensure Rose has on her best afternoon dress to receive visitors,' Mother said frostily. 'And remind her of the manners required for taking tea and conversing pleasantly.'

'Yes, Madam.'

Miss Parson scowled at Rose and towed her up the stairs.

'I don't have an afternoon dress,' Rose said, wanting to be as difficult as possible. What was the point of having a birthday when she was not allowed to go to the park and explore the stream and climb hills and play cricket?

Miss Parson opened the wardrobe and selected Rose's least favourite dress, one made of white lace and frills with a hundred tiny buttons down the back and on the long sleeves. It took forever to put on, and Rose usually spilt something on it within five minutes.

'This will do fine,' Miss Parson said.

Rose groaned, but with Miss Parson's help she put on the white dress and waited as the governess began buttoning the back.

'Stop pushing your shoulders forward,' Miss Parson said.

'I'm not!'

'Pull in your stomach then.'

Rose tried, but she could tell something was wrong. Miss Parson kept pulling and eventually she finished the buttoning, but Rose could hardly breathe.

'It's too short as well as tight. You must have

grown more than I realised,' Miss Parson said.

'I won't wear it then,' Rose said.

'It's your best day dress. It will have to do.'

'But I won't have room to eat any of my birthday tea!'

There was a knock at the door, and Sally popped her head in. 'Your mother says to come now, Miss. The guests have arrived.'

Rose put on her new locket and went down the wide marble staircase, stopping on the landing. She checked there was no one in the hall below. Should she risk it? She perched on the polished curved rail and pushed off, her dress flying up, her face flushed. That was the fastest she'd ever gone! She jumped off and stumbled, then straightened.

'Rose!' Mother stood in the doorway of the drawing room, glaring. 'Is that any way for a lady to behave? And what on earth is wrong with that dress? Oh, never mind now. Come and greet your guests.'

They're not *my* guests, Rose thought crossly, but she followed her mother into the room. Grandmother was already seated in the best armchair, and Aunt Philippa was inspecting Mother's latest ornaments and figurines.

'Felicitations,' boomed Uncle Charles. He bent down to kiss Rose, his whiskers prickling her cheeks, his fob watch falling out of his pocket and dangling on its chain. 'Got a little present for you, Rosie,' he whispered.

Rose brightened. Uncle Charles understood how hard it was to be good all the time. His gifts were usually exactly the kind of thing she wanted. Last year he'd given her a world map.

'Happy birthday, Rose,' Grandmother said. Her face was almost as stern as Miss Parson's, and her black muslin dress with its high neck and long puffed sleeves made her seem even more severe. Rose knew better than to kiss Grandmother – a curtsey was required. She made it without wobbling too much and

Grandmother tapped her black fan on Rose's shoulder in approval.

When everyone had chosen their seat, Rose found one for herself in the corner. Immediately, the grownups began talking about Elspeth Brown who'd married beneath her, whatever that meant, and Harry Borland, who had a gambling problem. Rose hid a huge yawn behind her hand. Why on earth did grownups waste so much time gossiping?

She curled her fingers around the wooden end of the chair arm, imagining it was a cricket ball and she was lining up to bowl to Edward. That's probably what he was doing right at that moment – playing cricket at school.

Sally nudged open the door and, smiling at the birthday girl, carried in a huge cream cake decorated with sugar flowers and eleven candles.

Well, it wasn't a trip to the park, but Rose did love cake! Maybe Mother would let her have two pieces, just this once.

2

Buttons and Bustles

THE grownups' voices droned on, and the
cream cake Rose had eaten sat heavily on
top of the sandwiches. Her eyelids drooped ...

'Rose!'

Her head jerked. 'Yes, Mother?'

'Tell Sally we need a fresh pot of tea, please.'

As Rose was leaving the drawing room, she
checked the mantel clock. With any luck, the
visitors would be gone in half an hour or so.

'She *what*?' Aunt Philippa screeched.

Rose's ears pricked up. She stopped outside
the door to listen.

'The letter came this morning,' Mother said. 'Even Daniel was taken aback.' Daniel was Father's name.

'She's such a disgrace,' Aunt Philippa said. 'Everyone must think so.'

Who was a disgrace? This part actually sounded quite interesting.

'Now, now,' Uncle Charles huffed. 'Alice has an adventurous spirit, that's all.'

Rose smiled. They were talking about Aunt Alice, Father's sister, who lived in New Zealand. She'd gone there last year to take up a position as a governess. Aunt Alice was younger than Father, only twenty-five, and lots of fun. She even had her own bicycle, which was now stored in their stables. Aunt Philippa was Mother's sister, and no fun at all.

'Surely you don't have to receive her,' Grandmother said.

'Unfortunately, it's worse than that,' Mother said. 'She will be staying here with us.'

Now Rose found it almost impossible to stay quiet. She peeked around the door. Aunt Alice here? She couldn't wait!

'Oh!' gasped Aunt Philippa. 'You mustn't tell anyone!'

'Don't be ridiculous,' Uncle Charles said. 'You can't hide a grown woman.'

'Well, I shan't be inviting her to attend any functions with me,' Mother said. 'I'm hoping she will quickly find a position with lodgings.'

'Hmph,' said Grandmother. 'Not if people hear what she's been up to.' She stood, leaning forward and straightening slowly, like a card table unfolding. 'It's time we were leaving.'

'Rose?' called Mother. 'Come and say goodbye to your guests!'

Rose waited a few seconds, then went back in. As the women said their goodbyes, Uncle Charles winked at her. 'I haven't forgotten your gift, Rosie.' He drew a small parcel out of his pocket and slipped it to her. 'Just for you.'

So it was something Mother wouldn't approve of! 'Thank you, Uncle Charles.' He bent down and Rose kissed him, trying to avoid his whiskers. She kept the parcel hidden while the grownups went out to the carriage, and then headed up the stairs to her room.

As she reached the top, Mother called, 'Tomorrow we shall see about the abominable state of your wardrobe, Rose.'

That meant shopping, which Rose liked about as much as she liked sewing. Hours spent being measured and then standing around waiting while Mother fingered fabrics and laces and ribbons and buttons. Mother and Martha were obsessed with the latest fashions, and were forever having new dresses made. Martha chose soft muslins and flowered silks, and always looked like an angel. Whereas Rose felt like a lump of suet and besides, how could anyone run properly with long, heavy skirts? What would an explorer use lace for? Nothing!

In her room, Rose locked the door. The small parcel was an odd shape, and quite heavy. She ripped off the paper. A magnifying glass! A good solid one, too. Perfect for examining fossils and reading the tiny print on her world map. She peered at an ant on her windowsill – she could even see its antennae.

'Rose!' Miss Parson was rattling the door handle. 'Open this door.'

Rose slid the magnifying glass under her mattress and unlocked the door. 'Goodness,' she said innocently, 'how did that lock itself?'

Miss Parson glared suspiciously around the room but could see nothing out of place. 'I'll help you with your buttons,' she said instead.

It was such a relief to be out of the tight dress. Rose took several enormous breaths until she felt normal again.

'You'll have to get used to it,' Miss Parson said. 'You're old enough for a corset now.'

'What?'

'All young ladies wear corsets,' Miss Parson said. *All young ladies* was her favourite beginning to most sentences.

Not me, Rose thought. Nobody's going to make me wear something stupid like that.

It wasn't until she lay in bed that night that Rose remembered the conversation about Aunt Alice. When would she arrive? Ships from New Zealand took days to cross the Tasman Sea, and Rose wasn't sure how far Aunt Alice lived from the nearest port.

Perhaps she had to battle her way through the thick bush and fight the natives, all while carrying her own trunk and riding a horse astride like a man. Rose hugged herself with excitement. That was the kind of thing she imagined Aunt Alice doing, because she was so strong and brave.

And it was exactly the kind of thing Mother hated. She said Aunt Alice was an embarrassment to the family, and called her a 'bluestocking', which Rose thought sounded interesting. Maybe now that Aunt Alice would be staying with them, she could find out what it meant.

After just one hour of French lessons the next morning, Rose was desperate to get out of the small, stuffy schoolroom. It had been a spare bedroom once, and it was only when Father's business began to improve again after the Bust that Rose's family could afford a governess, and they had turned it into a schoolroom.

Rose couldn't remember the Bust, but she'd heard many times how lots of people had lost money, and thousands had left Melbourne to go and pan for gold in the West, hoping to get rich. It sounded like a terrible time. Mother had been forced to teach Edward and Martha by herself in the drawing room. Mother's patience was extremely short, and lessons had often only lasted an hour before she gave up. It was Martha who'd taught Edward and Rose to read and do sums.

Now Martha attended a finishing school and Edward was enrolled at a boys' college, and Rose was stuck at home with Miss Parson, who was supposed to turn her into a lady.

Sally knocked on the schoolroom door. 'Mrs McCubbin wishes Rose to be ready in ten minutes to go out.'

'Very well,' Miss Parson said. 'Rose, go and wash your face, and put your boots on.'

Rose did as she was told, hoping they were going to the park, but knowing in her heart that they wouldn't be. Sure enough, Mother announced they were going to Father's shop, McCubbin's Emporium. 'You need a complete new wardrobe,' Mother said.

Rose groaned. 'It's only that silly dress that's too small.'

'Nonsense,' Mother said as she retied the

large hat bow under her chin.

Out on the driveway, John waited with the family carriage. The horse stood placidly, and Rose longed to go and pat it, but ladies didn't do that. In fact, ladies never did anything interesting or exciting.

On their way into Bourke Street in the city, they passed a cable tram clanking along. Rose gazed at the people sitting on the open seats – she'd love to ride on a tram, but Mother thought they were 'common', which meant only poor people used them.

When they reached the front door of McCubbin's Emporium, Father was nowhere to be seen. I bet he's hiding, Rose thought with a grin. Martha had once told Rose that Father dreaded Mother's visits because she always criticised the goods he stocked.

It was Mother who insisted that, when Father expanded his drapery three years before, he rename it an Emporium. She had been most unhappy when Father began selling ready-made clothing to the working classes during the hard years after the Bust, but Father had ignored her. It'd kept the business going, he said, when all around were failing.

Mother whisked Rose past the linen and household goods on the ground floor, and up the stairs to where the tables were piled high with colourful bolts of material and rolls of lace. She sent Rose off with Miss Smith, whose white hair matched her starched white muslin blouse. Tape measures were draped around her neck.

Rose had to undress behind a curtain down to her chemise and bloomers, and stand still while Miss Smith measured every part of her, and wrote the numbers in her notebook. 'There,' she said, smiling. 'Aren't you excited to be getting lovely new dresses?'

'I want to ride a bicycle,' Rose said, 'and run and jump and play cricket. I can't do any of those things dressed in fancy lace and satin.

Maybe you could measure me for pantaloons.'

'Oh.' Miss Smith looked worried. 'I'm not sure you're –'

'Rose,' Mother called from the other side of the curtain. 'Are you finished?'

'Yes.' Hopefully, Mother had already ordered everything and they could go home now. But Mother showed Rose every single bolt of material and roll of lace she had chosen, with Miss Smith draping coloured lengths all over her as if she were a Christmas tree, while they talked endlessly about buttons and bustles.

Holy smoke! thought Rose. I could have climbed Kilimanjaro twice in the time I've been standing here. Father had told Rose that Mount Kilimanjaro was the highest mountain in Africa. Rose imagined standing on top, the clouds below her and the sun warm on her face.

However, just when it seemed like the clothes torture was over, Rose discovered there was worse to come.

Miss Smith held up a funny piece of underwear with buttons down the front and two straps. The back was laced loosely together, and the waist curved inwards. A corset! Rose edged back but Mother pushed her forward again. 'Go and try it on, Rose,' she said.

'But . . .' The corset looked tiny – far too small to be comfortable.

'It gives a lovely shape,' Miss Smith said.

Before Rose knew it, she was back behind the curtain, and Mother watched while Miss Smith put the corset on her and pulled the laces tight, one at a time.

Within moments, Rose was gasping for breath, her face burning red.

'Lovely,' said Miss Smith.

'Much better,' said Mother, smiling at last. 'We'll take that as well.'

Rose gaped at her mother. Even a suit of armour would be more comfortable than the corset. Well, she'd just refuse to wear it!

3

Aunt Alice Arrives!

AFTER waiting for Mother to finish her orders, Rose climbed into the carriage and wriggled, exhausted, into the corner seat. As they headed off, they passed Coles Arcade, but she could barely raise the energy to look at the tempting rainbow signs and window displays. They stocked more books than anywhere else in Melbourne, and she'd heard there were amazing things inside like monkeys and parrots. But Coles Arcade was another place that Mother said wasn't fit to be seen in. Rose sighed. If Mother wasn't so high and mighty, life would be a lot more entertaining.

When they arrived home, there were three trunks and two large hatboxes in the hallway. Aunt Alice had arrived!

Just as Mother was demanding to know where the clutter had come from, a familiar voice floated down the stairs. 'Elizabeth, I'm so sorry about the luggage. We weren't sure which room I was to stay in.'

'Aunt Alice!' Rose called. 'Hello!'

Next to her, Rose heard Mother hiss to Sally, 'I told you the small room on the third floor.'

'Miss Alice said she wouldn't fit in there, Madam,' Sally whispered.

Mother made a snorting noise and Rose had great trouble keeping her giggles inside her.

'Hello, Rose. You've grown so much!' Aunt Alice galloped down the stairs and swept Rose up in a huge hug.

'Aunt Alice!' Rose said. 'You're wearing …'

'Pantaloons,' Aunt Alice said. 'They're the latest fashion for adventurous outings.'

'Not if I can help it,' Mother said icily.

'I'm sure I can settle into the green room next to Rose's,' Aunt Alice said. 'Could John take my luggage up, please?'

John avoided Mother's glare and heaved the first trunk onto his shoulder, escaping up the staircase.

Rose's stomach gave an enormous rumble. 'Mother, I'm starving. Can we have lunch?'

'I'm sure Cook has it ready, Rose. Let's go into the dining room and I'll ring the bell.' Mother marched off without another word to Aunt Alice, who didn't seem to mind a bit. She winked at Rose. 'I can see I'm as welcome as a downpour in December.'

'Come and eat lunch with us,' Rose said, taking her hand. 'Mother will be all right once she gets used to you again.'

'What about you, Rose? Could you get used to me again?'

'Oh, very much.'

At the dining table, Rose sat and inspected Aunt Alice over the salt and pepper shakers. There was something different about her. It wasn't just her tanned skin, when all the ladies in Melbourne kept theirs pale under parasols. Her face was sharper, her eyes flashed instead of just shining. And her hair was pulled back into a tight knot instead of piled on her head. In her pantaloons and flannel blouse, she looked . . . strong. Not delicate and ladylike at all.

Rose imagined herself looking just like Aunt Alice, and a little thrill ran through her. She had a feeling life was going to be quite different with Aunt Alice in the house.

Rose poked her fork into the sliced tongue on her plate. It was grainy and tough, so she hid it under her potatoes. Mother was silent, picking her way through her lunch, eyes fixed on the tablecloth in front of her.

Aunt Alice smiled at Rose. 'How is school?'

'I'm not allowed to go to school,' Rose said. 'I have a governess, Miss Parson.'

'That's a shame,' Aunt Alice said.

Rose saw her mother stiffen and her eyebrows arrow down. Normally, that was a signal to be quiet, but Rose was too curious. 'Why? I thought you were a governess in New Zealand.'

'That's why I went,' Aunt Alice said. 'But the position didn't work out. The girls' mother was very ... difficult.' She smiled. 'So another governess and I started our own school.'

'Your own school?' Rose said. 'That's wonderful! Then why have you come back to Melbourne?'

Mother's fork clattered onto the plate, but Aunt Alice took no notice, leaning towards Rose. 'Apparently I was teaching young ladies inappropriate lessons. There was a campaign against me, and lots of people withdrew their daughters from the school.'

'Inappropriate?' The word burst out of Mother. 'That's a strange word to use. I heard it was dangerous and . . . *masculine*!'

What on earth could Mother mean? How could a girls' school be dangerous? Maybe the girls sailed ships and swam at the beach and played cricket. 'What did you teach them?' asked Rose.

'All about politics, and how to vote.' Alice raised her eyebrows at Rose. 'You do know that New Zealand was the first country to let women vote in elections. It's only fair that everyone gets to choose who is in charge. Everywhere else it's just the men who decide!'

Rose made a face. She had heard Father talk about voting and politics, and they didn't sound dangerous or exciting to her.

'Huh!' Mother said. 'Women don't need to

vote. Men run Victoria perfectly well.'

'Run Victoria well?' Aunt Alice said, her voice steely. 'I suppose that was why we had the Bust, and all those people starved and lost their savings.'

Mother threw her napkin onto the table. 'I will not be insulted in my own house. I will finish my lunch later.' She stood and swept towards the door, then paused. 'Rose, bring your plate. You can eat in the schoolroom.'

Aunt Alice smiled and mouthed, 'Go on.'

Rose picked up her plate and followed her mother up the stairs. What was so bad about what Aunt Alice had said? She was dying to know more about this extraordinary school.

In the schoolroom, Rose quickly scraped the tongue into the bin, covering it with some scrap paper. Her stomach was still only half-full. I know! she thought. I'll sneak down to the kitchen and ask Cook for a big slice of apple pie!

4
Small Secrets

*a*s Rose pushed open the kitchen door, she goggled at the sight of Aunt Alice sitting at the large wooden table with a cup of tea in front of her, chatting with Cook and Sally while John stood near the wood stove, smiling.

Aunt Alice waved her closer. 'Shut the door, Rosie. We don't want your mother barging in.'

Rose did as she was told, and her stomach rumbled. 'Is there any apple pie left?' she asked.

'Of course,' Cook said, and cut Rose an enormous piece. It was brown and crunchy on top, with delicious soft apple and cinnamon inside.

The others were talking about the Emporium. Rose screwed up her nose. 'It's an awful place. They sell corsets!'

Much to Rose's disgust, the adults all laughed. 'Sorry, Rose,' Aunt Alice said, wiping her eyes. 'We're not laughing at you. It was the expression on your face. I take it you don't like corsets?'

'You can't breathe in them!' Rose eyed her aunt. 'Do you wear one?'

'No, I do not,' Aunt Alice said. 'Another black mark against me, no doubt!'

A bell jangled loudly from its rack on the wall. 'That's Mrs McCubbin,' said Sally. 'She'll be wanting something.'

'I'd better go back upstairs,' Rose said.

'I'll come with you,' Aunt Alice said. 'Do you want to help me unpack? I have some souvenirs of New Zealand that might interest you.'

'Yes, please,' Rose said, jumping up.

Rose and Aunt Alice crept up the stairs and, once in Aunt Alice's bedroom, they closed and locked the door. John had stacked Alice's three trunks neatly along the wall and she bent to open the first one, pulling out all of the clothes. There were only three dresses and a nightgown, plus some underwear. Rose peered into the trunk. It was filled with books!

'Do you have your own library?' Rose asked, reaching for the top book before she could stop herself.

'You can't teach properly without good books,' Aunt Alice said. 'You may borrow any of these.'

Rose's hand faltered. Already she could see some boys' adventure stories that Mother wouldn't approve of. Guilt prickled over her skin. Mother was very strict about what Rose was allowed to read. Rose had a funny feeling that trouble was coming, but how could she possibly turn down the offer of such fascinating books? There was one about Africa, one about fish and one with the mysterious title of *The Jungle Book*. Underneath that lay another book that Rose had been longing to read since Edward told her about it – *Treasure Island*!

'May I read this? Please?'

'Of course,' Aunt Alice said. 'It's a ripping story. In fact, why don't you keep it? Let's make it your birthday present. Or a part of it, anyway.'

'Thank you so much! I'll be happy just with this.' Rose hugged the book to her chest.

'You shouldn't be so easily pleased, Rose,' Aunt Alice said, a glint in her eyes.

'What do you mean?'

'I think your mother has –' A sharp rap at the door cut her off.

'Rose McCubbin! Are you in there?' It was Miss Parson. 'It's time for your piano practice.'

'Yes,' Rose squeaked. In a panic, she looked

around for somewhere to hide her precious book.

Aunt Alice held out her hand. 'I'll give it to you later, after my suffragette meeting.'

'What's a suffragette, Aunt Alice?' asked Rose.

'Suffragettes are women, like me, who think we should be able to do the same things as men,' said Aunt Alice as she unlocked the door. It swung wide open to reveal Miss Parson looking huffy. 'Miss Parson, how would you like to become a suffragette?' Alice asked.

Miss Parson paled and stepped back as if Alice had a disease that she didn't want to catch. 'And march all over town demanding to be allowed to vote? I could think of nothing worse. How uncouth. Come along, Rose.' She marched off down the corridor.

Rose said goodbye to Aunt Alice and trailed after the stiff-backed governess. A whole hour of pounding the piano keys! How much more exciting to be curled up on her bed, reading

Treasure Island. Miss Parson was in such a cross mood that Rose ended her practice with stinging fingers from raps with a wooden ruler. As soon as she was allowed, Rose ran out of the piano room, down the stairs, and into the garden.

Beyond the stables were an orchard and a vegetable patch. The apple trees were laden with fruit. Rose climbed into the lower branches and picked a large, juicy apple, sinking her teeth into it. Maybe I could fetch my new book, and read it here, under the tree in the autumn sunshine, she thought. And then she could hide it in the secret box she kept in a hole behind the ivy on the wall. Maybe she should put her cricket ball and her lovely magnifying glass there, just for safekeeping, away from Miss Parson's big, snooping nose. Rose closed her eyes and breathed in the smell of grass and fallen apples and late-blooming roses. There was a rustle below her.

'What are you doing out here?'

It was Edward, hands in his pockets, staring up at her. He must've just arrived home.

'Hiding from Miss Parson. And Mother.'

Edward climbed up and sat on another branch, picking an apple and munching with his mouth open. Rose was about to remind him to close it when she realised that would make her sound like Mother. 'What did you do at school today?'

Edward scowled. 'Nothing. It was boring.'

'How could school ever be boring? You should be here with Miss Parson. You could embroider a tablecloth or two.'

Edward laughed. 'No thanks. But school isn't as exciting as you think.'

Rose didn't believe him. Martha's finishing school sounded horrendous – just imagine learning how to run a household all day! – but the boys' school must be marvellous. Rose could see herself reading about darkest Africa, or learning about ancient Rome. 'Do you play cricket with the other boys?' she asked Edward.

'No,' he said, hunching his shoulders.

Rose was puzzled. Judging by his expression, Edward's school seemed worse than Martha's. She wanted to cheer him up. 'Thanks awfully for the cricket ball, Ed. I know it was your favourite.'

'That's all right. You're darned good at bowling, you know – especially for a girl.' He grimaced. 'Sorry about those horrible cherries – Mother made me. Have you got the ball with you? We could play catch.' He finished his apple and threw the core away.

'No, it's in my room. Hide-and-seek? I'll let you hide first.'

'Hide-and-seek is a baby's game,' he said. Then he grinned. 'Make sure you count to fifty, and don't look!' He climbed down and ran towards the stables. Rose giggled, closed her eyes and started counting.

5

News and Views

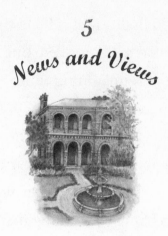

ROSE and Edward got to play two games of hide-and-seek before they were called inside. Too late, Rose remembered that she'd been going to retrieve her tin box of special things from behind the ivy, and put her book into it. She would have to leave *Treasure Island* with Aunt Alice. There was nowhere in her room that was safe from Miss Parson, who came and searched through Rose's drawers and cupboards regularly, although Rose could never work out why. Miss Parson did it when Rose wasn't there, but she left telltale signs – little things out of place, bedcovers a bit crooked. But Mother had told her she was imagining things when Rose had mentioned it.

Maybe Miss Parson thought she was hiding a beau! Rose giggled. She wasn't at all interested in boys, except to play cricket with. Martha had had two handsome young men call on her already, probably because she was so pretty and graceful. Rose hoped Martha wouldn't do something silly like get married. Rose would miss her too much.

As she ran through the gardens, Rose waved to the gardener who kept everything so neat and tidy. There were freshly mowed lawns spreading in every direction, perfectly trimmed hedges and square garden beds with precise rows of flowers. Even the fountain at the front of the house had been scrubbed clean.

She gazed up at the big arched windows and caught a glimpse of Aunt Alice moving about in her bedroom. Perhaps she would come out and play some cricket later? Aunt Alice looked like she'd make a fine batsman.

Rose swung her arm over as if she was bowling a spinner to Aunt Alice, and skipped inside, whistling cheerily to herself.

'Rose!' Mother called. 'Stop that at once. Ladies do not whistle!'

'Yes, Mother.' Rose ran up the stairs as fast as she could and burst into Aunt Alice's bedroom, startling her aunt into dropping the pile of freshly laundered stockings she was carrying.

'Sorry!' Rose knelt and picked up the stockings, bundling them all together. As she handed the mess back to her aunt, she said, 'But none of these are blue.'

Aunt Alice laughed, and sat on her bed to sort and match the stockings properly. 'No, they're all sensible black. Why?'

Rose blushed. 'Mother said you were a . . . bluestocking. Is that a rude thing to say?'

'Not really,' Aunt Alice said. 'Bluestockings are the kind of women who go to university and study, and read lots of interesting books.'

Rose's eyes widened. 'Did you go to university?

'No, but I did attend a very good girls' school in London. I was lucky – I learnt a lot there.'

'Mother said women are no good at learning because their brains are too small.'

Aunt Alice spluttered. 'Oh my goodness, Rose, things for you are worse than I could ever have imagined!'

Rose edged back towards the door, her face burning. She couldn't bear Aunt Alice thinking she was stupid and babyish. But Aunt Alice leapt up and rushed towards Rose, enveloping her in a big hug.

'I'm sorry, Rosie, I didn't mean to hurt your feelings.' She kissed Rose on the tip of her nose. 'Will you forgive me?'

Rose was overwhelmed by the warmth of the

hug and the feeling of loving arms around her. It took her a long moment to answer. 'Of course.'

'Good.' Aunt Alice drew back and searched Rose's face. 'It is not your fault that your mother tells you such nonsense – after all, it's what lots of people still believe. In fact, I think you are the kind of girl who would do very well at the University. What would you like to study?'

Rose's eyes lit up. 'Geography, and maybe history, and I want to know about insects and plants, and fossils too, and how things work. Like those new motor cars – have you seen them? Father is thinking of buying one. I'd love to try driving. But I'm not even allowed on a bicycle.'

'That's a wonderful list of subjects,' Aunt Alice said. 'As for the bicycle, you can always ride mine. Now, I'm going to give you something I've been saving for you.' She reached into one of the trunks and pulled out a strangely shaped wooden carving. It had big eyes and a long tongue that curled out of its mouth. She handed it to Rose, who ran her fingers over the smooth wood.

'It looks scary,' Rose said, 'but it feels lovely. What is it?'

'It's called a tiki, and it was carved for me by a Maori friend. It's a symbol of knowledge and inner strength.' She reached into the trunk again, and showed Rose a beautiful green spiral. 'This is a koru, and it's like a new fern uncurling. It can mean new beginnings. I thought it was perfect for me.'

'You have a friend who is a Maori?' Maori warriors were huge and carried spears and had tattoos – Rose had seen a drawing of one once. 'Aren't they ... ferocious?'

'They certainly used to be,' Aunt Alice said. 'But things are different in New Zealand now.'

Aunt Alice had seen and heard so many unusual and exciting things, and Rose wanted to know as much as possible. From downstairs came the clanging of the dinner bell. Rose

jumped up. 'Father is home! And I'm starving.'
It felt like days since the apple pie.

After Rose and Aunt Alice had washed their
hands and tidied their hair, they went down to
the dining room. Father was already seated at
the head of the table, quizzing Edward about
his schoolwork. 'And what have they told you
about the Boer War?'

Rose leaned in to listen. The Boer War
was going on in South Africa, which was a
long way from Mount Kilimanjaro – she'd
looked it up on her world map. Father had
told her that Boers were the people who had
gone to South Africa from Holland, and now
they were fighting against the British, who
had settled there too. Rose loved hearing
about Africa – even the name seemed full of
adventure – but the war sounded frightening.

'The stupid Boers just want all the gold for
themselves,' Edward said. 'It belongs to Britain.'

Father's bushy eyebrows rose up at Edward's

words. 'Poppycock, boy!' he shouted. 'Who told you that?'

Edward's face turned the colour of beets, and Rose and Aunt Alice hesitated in the doorway. 'Er, it was, it was . . . Robert Quinlan.'

'Is this Mr Quinlan a teacher?' Father boomed.

'N – no,' Edward said. 'He's a pupil.'

Father's eyebrows shot up again. 'If you prefer to listen to the ill-informed rubbish of a schoolboy instead of your teachers, then perhaps you should be instructed at home again, by Miss Parson.'

Rose cringed at his gruff tone, but she was even more astonished to see Edward brighten, as if he would rather stay at home with Miss Parson! Could Edward hate his school *that* much?

Just then, Mother arrived behind them. 'Sit down, Rose, for heaven's sake!' She swept past, ignoring Aunt Alice, who was receiving a hearty kiss from Father, and sat at the opposite end of the table. Immediately, she rang the small bell beside her plate.

Sally rushed in, carrying a tureen of steaming pea soup.

'Where is Martha?' Father said. 'Has she been called?'

'I'm here, Father.' Martha glided into the dining room gracefully. She glanced at Mother's stony face, then went over to kiss Aunt Alice. 'It's lovely to see you again.'

Aunt Alice also ignored Mother. 'Are you still painting those beautiful watercolours, Martha?'

Martha nodded as she sat down. 'And what are your plans, Aunt Alice?'

'I believe I will look for a post as a governess,' Aunt Alice replied, her eyes on her soup plate. 'Or perhaps a position in a school. Or . . . I could start my own school.'

'Hmph,' Mother said. Her spoon clattered against her plate.

For a moment, Father stared down the long table, past the candelabra, then said, 'You tried that in New Zealand. It failed. Word did get back here, you know.'

Aunt Alice smiled thinly, and Rose held her breath. Was an argument about to start? The pea soup stuck in her throat.

'I have returned with excellent letters of recommendation,' Aunt Alice said. 'And the school failed due to the lies told by two of the mothers.' Rose felt as if Aunt Alice was spearing Father with her eyes. 'You know about people who block good ideas, Daniel. Just look at Mr Lyne in New South Wales, trying to undermine Federation. Sometimes one person is all it takes.'

There was a sudden charged silence, as if lightning had struck the dinner table. Mother had gone pale, her fingers gripping her soup spoon so hard that Rose thought it might bend. Everyone else bent over their bowls and scraped away noisily. Rose puzzled over Aunt Alice's mention of Mr Lyne, who was in charge of New South Wales. Father said he was trying to influence people not to vote for Federation. Maybe those two mothers in New Zealand tried to turn everyone against Aunt Alice's school. Everyone seemed to be talking about Federation these days, and Rose thought joining all the states into one big country sounded pretty sensible.

Once Mother left the table, Father seemed more relaxed and asked Aunt Alice lots of questions about New Zealand. Rose, Martha and Edward were all totally entranced by Aunt Alice's stories. 'We canoed all the way down the Wanganui River – so much easier than overland,' she said. She'd even been mountain trekking and sailing.

Rose knew she'd love sailing and trekking up mountains. How could Aunt Alice bear to come back? Life here seemed so boring!

6
Speaking Up

THAT night, Rose tossed and turned, and finally fell asleep, only to dream of being at a ball and strapped into a corset so huge and tight that she toppled right over and couldn't breathe. She woke, gasping and crying, and found Aunt Alice next to her bed, trying to soothe her.

'Oh, thank goodness it wasn't real!' Rose described her dream and her new corset.

'No wonder you're having nightmares,' Aunt Alice said. 'A corset at your age? It's ridiculous. They're ridiculous at any age.'

'Mother loves corsets,' Rose said.

Aunt Alice shuddered. 'No doubt Martha is wearing them, too.'

'Hers is called the Bride's Dream. Wearing it is supposed to help you find a husband.'

Aunt Alice just shook her head.

'May I ask you a question?' Rose said.

'Of course, Rosie dear.' Aunt Alice held Rose's hands. 'Ask away.'

Rose felt her chin trembling but she got the words out all the same. 'Do you think I'm doomed? That I'll *have* to be like Martha when I'm older?'

'Good gracious, no! What makes you think that?' Aunt Alice's face creased with concern.

'You said I was in a terrible state. And I do feel terrible. Mother is always scolding me, even though anyone can see I'll never be as beautiful or ladylike as Martha.' A tear trickled down Rose's cheek, and Aunt Alice brushed it away.

'Rose, if I made you feel bad, I am ever

so sorry.' She leaned over and gave Rose a hug. 'I think you are a beautiful, intelligent, wonderful girl, and it pains me to think that your mother will condemn you to a life of new dresses and corsets and . . . learning from an addle-brain like Miss Parson! You should be at school with girls your own age.'

Rose knew in her heart that Aunt Alice was right, but she couldn't for the life of her see how she could stand up to Mother and win. It would be like climbing Mount Everest.

She didn't know how to answer Aunt Alice, so instead she slid down under her quilt and said, 'Thank you for coming in and comforting me. I think I can sleep now.'

'Oh. Jolly good, then.' Aunt Alice stood and looked down at Rose for a few long moments. Eventually, she smiled and bent to kiss Rose goodnight. 'We'll talk more tomorrow.'

However, the next morning, Aunt Alice wasn't at breakfast. Rose, puzzled, was marched off to the schoolroom by Miss Parson, where she spent the morning writing thank-you letters to her grandmother and aunt and uncle, and then embroidering her initials on three handkerchiefs. All the time, she thought longingly of *Treasure Island* hidden in Aunt Alice's room, and plotted how to fetch it.

When Aunt Alice wasn't there for lunch either, Rose had to ask Mother where she was.

'Looking for a new governess position.'

'Does that mean she'll leave us?' Rose said.

'I should hope so,' Mother snapped. 'Now, after lunch Mrs Alcott, the dressmaker, is bringing your new dresses for a fitting.'

'Oh.' Maybe later she could read her book.

The afternoon was long and awful. Rose had to wear the corset, which dug into her stomach, and stand in one spot being pushed and pulled and having pins stuck into her.

She was tired by the time the family went into the sitting room after dinner, and curled up next to the fire. Sally brought Father a snifter of brandy. Aunt Alice was quiet, reading her book in the corner.

'I believe you had morning tea with Mrs Jamieson, Alice,' Father said. 'And afternoon tea with Mrs Widbey-Farthing.'

'I did,' Aunt Alice said, her eyes on her book.

'Both fine families,' Father said. 'A governess position with either should suit you admirably.'

'It should.'

Rose wondered if she was the only person who heard the edge in Aunt Alice's voice. Edward was focused totally on the newspaper, and Martha was busy choosing coloured threads for her embroidered sampler. But Mother's mouth pursed as if she'd sucked on a lemon. 'Beggars can't be choosers, Alice!'

Aunt Alice's head snapped up and the look in her eyes was enough to make Mother shift in her chair. 'I am *not* a beggar.'

'Of course not,' Father said, trying to smooth things over. 'You should only take a position where you will be entirely happy.'

Mother sniffed. 'I would have thought a woman with a reputation and no chance of marriage might –'

Aunt Alice stood up so abruptly that her book flew across the carpet. Rose rushed to pick it up.

'Daniel, I think I will read upstairs.' Without another word, Aunt Alice rushed out of the room. Rose was sure she saw tears in her aunt's eyes, and Rose's heart thumped madly against her ribs. What was wrong? Surely Mother wasn't going to force Aunt Alice to leave? She stared at her mother's satisfied expression.

'You will regret the day you invited her to stay, Daniel,' Mother said. 'Without asking me, I might add.'

'I don't need to ask you, Elizabeth, and I'll thank you to remember it.'

A chilly silence fell over the room. Rose pretended to be interested in Martha's sampler so she wouldn't have to look at anyone. Mother was always bossy, and usually Father tolerated it with a joke or brushed it aside, but it seemed this time Mother had gone too far. Rose hated it when the family was in such an unhappy way. It hadn't been like this for a long time, not since the Bust when Mother was so upset and angry about being poor. Rose had been very small, but she could just remember her parents shouting and then their freezing silences.

Since Father's finances had improved and he'd bought this big house, Mother had been much happier, even though Father complained about the amount of money she spent. Now money was not a problem, but the arguments made Rose's stomach churn. She tried to thread a needle for Martha but her fingers were trembling so much that she had to give up.

Edward asked to be excused, saying he had schoolwork to do, and handed Father *The Argus* newspaper. Martha joined Mother, exclaiming over pictures of new hats in her fashion magazine that had come all the way from London.

'Come over here, Rose,' Father said. 'My eyes are tired tonight. Why don't you read the news to me?'

Rose was glad of something interesting to do, since she still wasn't able to read *Treasure Island*. She took the newspaper from Father and settled down beside him on the chaise under the gaslit chandelier. 'What shall I read?' she asked.

'Whatever takes your fancy, my love,' he said. 'I've read the financial pages already.'

Rose focused straight away on the few pictures, especially the one of the motor car. She began to read aloud. 'Mr Waldo Stutterfield announced today that he planned to import more motor cars from his factory in England, which has caused an outcry from those here who wish to see an Australian motor car being built. The Lewis Cycle and Motor Works in Adelaide is still working on their own motor car. The first Lewis machine is yet to come out of the Works, but early testing has proved entirely successful. Mr Lewis expects his first car to be on the road by Christmas.'

Father grunted and said, 'But will it match up to the Talbots and Daimlers? That's what I want to know.'

'Are you planning to buy a motor car, Father?' Rose jiggled in her seat. 'Oh, please do. I would so love to drive one!'

'Drive?' Father laughed uproariously. 'You're a bit small to drive a motor car, I'm afraid.'

'But when I'm older and bigger, I will.'

'You will not.' Mother's voice cut across the room. 'Ladies do not drive cars.'

Father's moustache twitched and, for a moment, Rose thought he was going to disagree with Mother, but he turned to Rose instead and said, 'If I buy one, you may ride in it. How about that?'

Rose opened her mouth, but she could feel Mother's eyes boring into her, so she just nodded. When I'm grown up, she thought, I'll have my own car and Mother *won't* be asked to ride in it.

She scanned the paper again. There were people in London talking about Federation – it seemed the British Parliament had to approve it. Rose skipped over that – there was something much more interesting on the Boer War, and a map of the vast plains in southern Africa. What if they were fighting the war and were attacked by . . . lions? Surely that might be possible? She began to read the article to Father. 'Lord Robert enters Kroonstad. The Boers in full retreat.'

'Rose, it's time you went to bed,' Mother said.

'But the news is about our soldiers,' she protested.

Mother used her most icy glare. 'Ladies don't need to know such matters.'

'Why not? We live in the world, too.'

Mother's mouth opened and closed, and a deep red flush filled her face. When she spoke, her voice was quiet and steely. 'I will not have you speak to me in that tone, Rose. Miss Parson has obviously not been doing her job at all well.'

The mention of Miss Parson was the final straw for Rose. She jumped to her feet, ignoring Father's restraining hand. 'Miss Parson is only good at snooping in my room and making me mend stupid stockings. Father seems to realise I have a brain in my head – why can't you?'

'Because in young ladies, manners will trump brains every time!' Mother snapped.

'Stop trying to turn me into Martha,' Rose said. 'I could think of nothing worse than spending my life hunting for a husband.'

'That's enough, Rose! How dare you talk about your sister in that way.' Mother stood, looming over Rose. 'Go to bed this minute, or else.'

'Oh, Martha, I didn't mean ...' But Martha just smiled sympathetically at Rose and shook her head slightly and, relieved, Rose rushed out of the sitting room and up the stairs.

Still, as she calmed down and thought about what had happened, Rose was convinced that she was right, even if Mother refused to see it. It would be wonderful to go to university, and then travel to Africa and China and other exotic places. She wasn't about to let either Miss Parson or Mother stop her, and an idea was beginning to form in her mind.

7
Fun in the City

ROSE had a restless sleep, and thankfully lessons the next morning were cut short when Miss Parson complained of a headache and had to lie down. Rose immediately went and knocked on Aunt Alice's door, hoping that she hadn't gone out again. But her aunt was home and she greeted Rose with a big smile.

'Just the person to brighten up my morning,' she said. 'Come in.'

Aunt Alice was still in her nightdress, with a beautiful silk kimono over the top. The material was soft and flowing, with pink and green butterflies all over it.

'No Miss Parson today?'

'She's ill,' Rose said. She hesitated. 'May I ask you something?'

'Of course.' Aunt Alice waited, her teacup cradled in her hands.

There was no point telling Aunt Alice about the scene with Mother, and Rose still felt guilty about her rudeness. But she needed help with the plan she'd worked out. 'I want to borrow your books,' she began.

'Of course. *Treasure Island* is there, and Mark Twain's stories are fun.'

'No, I mean all the other ones.' Rose pointed at the shelves against the wall. 'Maybe I could start with that *Smaller History of Greece*, and read the harder ones later.'

'You mean you want to teach yourself?' Aunt Alice's blue eyes were serious.

Rose felt shy. 'I'd really like it if you were

my governess,' Rose said. 'But you might be leaving soon.'

'I'll have to eventually,' said Aunt Alice. She sipped her tea and gazed out of the window. 'I need to earn a living, and not rely on your father to support me.'

'But he has pots of money! He doesn't mind.'

'No, but your mother does.' Aunt Alice smiled wryly. 'I think that's a wonderful idea, Rose. You can borrow any books you like, and you can discuss them with me. But, you know, the ideal would be for your mother to send you to school.'

'I so wish she would! Why is Mother so . . .' Rose couldn't think of a polite way to say it.

'Upset with you? With me?'

Rose nodded.

'Do you know where your mother's family comes from?' Aunt Alice asked.

'England?' Rose wasn't sure. She knew

Grandmother and Aunt Philippa were the only members of the family remaining. Grandfather had died a long time ago.

'Yes. Your grandfather was very rich, and then he lost all his money and died of a heart problem. Philippa had already married your uncle Charles, who was even richer, so he ended up supporting all of them.'

Uncle Charles really is kind, Rose thought.

'Your mother was engaged to marry a lord in London, but he called off the wedding when her family went broke. So Charles came to Australia with Philippa and your mother, and has done even better here.'

Rose couldn't believe it. 'Mother was meant to marry a lord in London? What about Father?'

As if realising she had said too much, Aunt Alice bit her bottom lip. 'Let's just say that your mother has had some big disappointments, and sometimes she wishes her life were different. Really, she just wants the best for you.'

'It doesn't seem like it,' Rose said. 'I'm not allowed to do anything interesting. I haven't even got anyone to play cricket with. And I'm good at it, Aunt Alice, really I am – even Edward says so.'

'I'd love to see you play. Perhaps one day we could all have a game. Now, is your mother going out today?'

'Yes, she's joined the Temperance Union and they have a luncheon every Friday.'

'Ah yes,' Aunt Alice said. 'The society of ladies who want to stop men drinking alcohol. They'd be better off putting their good works into getting the vote.' She put her cup down with a clatter. 'Never mind that. I'll tell John to get the buggy ready, and after your mother has left we'll go into town. And I know what we'll do – I'll take you to a coffee palace for lunch. It'll be your extra birthday present.'

'Really?' Rose jumped up and hugged her aunt. 'That will be marvellous. I've never been to a coffee palace. May I have whatever I want to eat?'

'Of course you may. Now go and find something to wear that you like, and we'll be ready to leave when the coast is clear.'

A question niggled at Rose. 'Are we not going to tell Mother?'

'Do you want to?' Aunt Alice asked. 'You know she will probably forbid you to go.'

Rose hunched her shoulders. 'Yes. But . . .'

'We could stop by the Emporium and ask your father to come with us. How about that?'

'Yes.' Rose smiled. She'd love to go out with Father and Aunt Alice together – away from Mother, Father was jolly good fun.

Rose put on her best green serge dress, one that still fitted her comfortably, and her boots, and a straw hat that sat on her curls. She tucked her gloves in a bag with a handkerchief and went downstairs. Aunt Alice was already in the hallway, talking to Sally.

'So she usually arrives home around three o'clock?'

Sally nodded. 'John's bringing the horse and buggy around from the stables. The mistress went in someone else's carriage today.'

Aunt Alice and Rose climbed in, and John sat at the front and took the reins. They were soon trotting towards the city, past large houses like theirs, then down the hill past smaller ones, and along Burwood Road, which was lined with shops and hotels. Aunt Alice said, 'Even in a year, this place has changed. The city grows bigger and bigger.'

As they swung around a corner, Rose pointed up the street. 'Look! A tram. I'd love to ride on one of those.'

'We can certainly do that,' said Aunt Alice. She tapped John on the shoulder. 'Stop by the next tram station. Rose wants to ride on a tram.'

John grinned. 'Would you like me to follow you into town, then?'

'No, thank you, we can hire a cab to bring us home.'

Rose stared at her aunt in astonishment. 'Do you mean it? I can really ride on the tram?'

'It's only a tram, Rose, not an elephant. Although an elephant sways as much.' Rose goggled at the thought of Aunt Alice riding an elephant. What fun! They clambered out of the buggy and Aunt Alice waved at the tram driver as the machine clanked closer and closer. 'Inside or out?'

'Outside,' Rose said. 'I want to watch the grip man.'

When the tram came to a squeaking stop, they climbed aboard. Aunt Alice faced outwards and Rose knelt on the wooden seat, watching as the driver clanged the bell, gripped the huge levers in the centre between the seats and pushed one forward. Below the tram, the hook grabbed onto the cable under the road and the tram took off with a jerk.

Luckily, Rose was expecting it and she hung on tightly.

The grip man saluted her cheerily and then went back to concentrating on his levers. Rose turned around and sat next to her aunt. 'This is so jolly. I'd like to be a grip man when I grow up.' She laughed at Aunt Alice's startled expression. 'Don't worry, I know I wouldn't be strong enough. I still want to drive a car, though. Father said he might buy one.'

'You should definitely learn to drive then,' Aunt Alice said. 'But don't forget about university.'

'That's why I'm going to teach myself,' Rose said. 'Nobody studies embroidery and letter writing at university.'

'Martha and Edward are both at school. I'm sure you will go, too, one day.' She nudged Rose. 'Never forget, Rose, that your life is actually very privileged. At least you will never live like those people over there.'

Rose looked across the street and sucked in a breath. A family was standing outside a rundown house, with their worn and broken belongings piled on the muddy path. The mother was arguing with a man, shouting and tearing her hair. Her three children clung to her skirts, crying loudly.

'Are they being made to leave their house?' Rose asked. Aunt Alice nodded.

'That's dreadful,' Rose whispered. 'Can't we help?'

'That same thing happens many times every day,' Aunt Alice said. 'When you are poor, you have no right to anything, not even a roof over your head.'

'Watch the corner!' the grip man called, and everyone held on tight as the tram swung around on the track.

Rose was silent for a few moments. 'Is that how Mother felt, when her father lost all his money and they were poor in London?'

'Quite possibly. Although she would not have been shouting and crying in public. But alone, in her room, feeling embarrassed and angry, thinking that everyone was talking about her ... yes, I think so.'

'Oh.' Rose was quiet for the rest of the journey, enjoying the tram and the world gliding past. At the last stop, the grip man asked her if she'd like to ring the bell, and she jumped up on the seat to pull the rope. Clang, clang!

'That was the best part of all,' she told her aunt when they got off the tram in Collins Street. It had rained earlier, and the horses and carts, hansom cabs and carriages splashed through the puddles. Rose marvelled at the tall buildings – some were more than eight storeys high!

They made their way to the McCubbin Emporium in Bourke Street, and climbed to the top floor, to Father's office.

'What a delightful interruption,' he said,

coming out from behind his huge wooden desk. He kissed them both. 'What can I do for you?'

'I'm taking Rose out to luncheon for her birthday, which I missed. We hoped you'd come with us.'

Father sighed. 'I'm sorry, I can't. I have an important meeting shortly.' He ruffled Rose's hair and straightened. 'Alice, I hope you didn't take offence at Elizabeth's ... comments.'

Aunt Alice smiled brightly, but Rose could see it was forced. 'It's fine, Daniel. But I have my heart set on my own school one day, and working as a governess for women who think in such opposite ways to myself is something I cannot bring myself to do. I hope you won't mind if I stay on with you a little longer.'

Father gave Aunt Alice a kiss on her cheek. 'As long as you want to. You know how much I enjoy your company.'

'Thank you.' She smiled at Rose, this time a genuine smile. 'Let's go and indulge ourselves.'

'I recommend Parer's Crystal Palace,' Father said. 'Their beef is the best in town.'

'Then that is where we'll go,' Aunt Alice announced.

It wasn't until they were standing back on Bourke Street that Aunt Alice said, 'I was hoping he'd say that. Your mother wouldn't approve, but it's your father's idea. Perfect!'

Rose nodded excitedly, pushing away the familiar uneasy feeling.

Parer's wasn't far from the Emporium. It was a four-storey building with a cafe, billiard rooms, private dining rooms, accommodation and a saloon. As Aunt Alice steered Rose into the cafe, she gaped at her surroundings – walls lined with framed mirrors, furniture covered in plush materials, thick velvet curtains draping the windows and fountains trickling water while music played.

A waitress seated them at a table and Aunt Alice read the menu.

'Have anything you fancy,' she said.

'Not tongue,' Rose said, 'or quail or oysters.' She inspected what the customers at other tables were eating. 'That looks nice. What is it?'

Aunt Alice asked the waitress.

'That's a Chinese dish, Madam,' she said, frowning at Rose. 'The little girl might not like it.'

'What's in it?' Rose asked.

'Chicken. Vegetables. A black sauce made from beans.' The waitress shrugged. 'Some customers say it's real tasty.'

'I'll have that,' Rose said. 'And peach pie.'

'I'll have the same,' said Aunt Alice.

'Really?' Rose asked. 'It might taste awful.'

'Couldn't be any worse than boiled mutton. And a sight better than tongue.'

Rose couldn't stop staring at all the grand decorations. Paintings of woodlands and fox hunts, golden cherubs with wings in the corners, even striped wallpaper. Above them, a chandelier sparkled like jewels. 'How beautiful,' she whispered.

'It's an electric one,' Aunt Alice said. 'Not gas, like your lights at home.'

'Father wants to put electricity in,' Rose said, 'but Mother says she doesn't like it. She should come here and see how wonderful it looks.'

Aunt Alice laughed. 'I don't think your mother would set foot in here.'

'Why not?'

'This coffee palace has a licence to sell alcohol, and as a member of the Temperance Union, she'd see this as a place of sin.'

Rose leaned back in her chair, feeling sick. 'We mustn't tell her I was here!'

'I won't, don't worry.' Aunt Alice frowned. 'Rose . . . I'm not trying to get you into trouble with your mother, but . . . I suspect it's going to happen anyway.'

'I'm always in trouble,' Rose said, fidgeting

with the edge of the embroidered tablecloth. 'I'm not graceful and elegant like Martha. I'd like to take that stupid corset and throw it in the Yarra.'

Aunt Alice sighed. 'I'm convinced the things make you ill and, at the very least, damage your ribs and back bone.'

The waitress arrived at their table, carrying two large plates of steaming food. 'Here you go, Miss. I hope you like it.' She sounded doubtful, but Aunt Alice smiled up at her.

'It smells delicious. Almost as good as frogs' legs or French garlic snails.'

The waitress looked at her as if she were mad. Rose giggled. 'Have you really eaten frogs' legs and snails?'

'Not yet, but I might one day.' Aunt Alice picked up her fork and speared a piece of chicken. 'However, I have eaten Chinese food, and I know how tasty it is. Have some, Rose – you did choose it, after all.'

Rose tasted her chicken tentatively, and smiled. 'It's scrumptious! It tastes like ... nothing I've ever eaten before.' She tucked into the plate full of chicken and multi-coloured vegetables with gusto, and finished before Aunt Alice was halfway through.

'Ooh,' said Rose, 'that was so good.'

8
Coles Arcade

'WHILE I'm finishing my lunch,' Aunt Alice said, 'you can think about where you'd like to go afterwards. The second half of your birthday treat. Anywhere you like. Even the public library, if you want to.'

Rose thought of all the thousands of books there, and the reading room and the big statues outside. Then she thought of the Botanical Gardens, with the lake and the little bridge. What about the Eastern markets – she'd heard they had fortune tellers who could tell your future. Then she knew exactly where she wanted to go.

'Coles Arcade,' she said. She added, 'And we definitely can't tell Mother.'

It was Aunt Alice's turn to smile and nod.

Rose couldn't quite believe she was going to walk right inside Coles Arcade and see everything she'd heard about! She wanted to leap around like a circus acrobat.

Over the front entrance arched a huge rainbow, and in the window was a display of the famous Funny Picture Books. Rose stopped for a moment to gaze in, then stepped over the threshold. What a sight! Rows and rows and rows of books, with ladders to climb to the highest shelves, and comfortable chairs to sit and read in. Signs said 'Read for as long as you like – nobody asked to buy'. There was even a magical toy hen that laid eggs.

'Do you want to try?' Aunt Alice asked.

'Ooh, yes, please.' Rose took a penny from her aunt and dropped it into the slot on the hen. There were clicks and whirring noises, a noisy clucking and ping! A small metal tin shaped like an egg dropped out of the hen.

'Goodness!' Rose said, picking it up. She prised the egg open and inside lay some little round sweets, one of which she popped into her mouth. 'Mmm, strawberry.'

Rose was just putting the tin in her little bag when she noticed a large cage, and something skimming back and forth on a swing. Was it a parrot? She peered into the cage and her mouth fell open. 'It can't be true. I'm dreaming.' She turned to Aunt Alice, hopping up and down with excitement. 'It's a monkey, a real live monkey!'

Aunt Alice nodded. 'There are some more on the top floor, and some beautiful parrots behind all those ferns. I tell you what,' she said, 'why don't you go and look at everything to your heart's content, and I will be over there in the poetry section.'

Rose was too excited to answer. She rushed

off to explore. Yes, there were more monkeys that chattered, and a cockatoo with a yellow plume that squawked, 'Read a book! Read a book!' She climbed one of the tall shelf ladders and looked all the way down the arcade, past rows and rows of books with funny signs above them.

When a big clock chimed three, Aunt Alice came to fetch Rose. 'We need to leave. Your mother will be home soon, and we should arrive before her if we can.' At Rose's crestfallen face, she said, 'Don't worry, I'm sure we'll be back another day.'

Aunt Alice led the way out and stood at the edge of the footpath to wave down a cab. Rose, still thinking about the books and the monkeys, barely noticed a carriage roll past and a woman leaning out, a look of fury on her face. But Aunt Alice stiffened, and murmured, 'Oh, dear.'

'What's the matter?' Rose asked.

'The woman in that carriage,' she said, pointing at it as it rolled up Bourke Street and around the corner. 'I think that was ... your mother!'

Rose gasped. 'Holy smoke! She saw us?'

Aunt Alice nodded, her mouth in a grim line. 'I'm afraid she did.'

9
Caught Out!

AUNT Alice hailed a cab and they sped up Bourke Street, the horse's mane and tail flying, as if it knew they were trying to beat Mother home.

Rose dared to hope that they would indeed get there first. Trees and houses whipped past, and as the horse slowed on the hill up from the river, Aunt Alice leaned out and peered ahead. 'There's the carriage.' She called up to the driver. 'Take the next right, and then the left. Hurry!'

The driver followed Aunt Alice's directions,

urging the horse on, and Rose realised they'd be entering their street from the other end. She leaned forward, craning her neck.

If they were caught, Rose'd be writing lines for the next year! What would Aunt Alice's punishment be? What if Mother put her out on the street? With all her trunks?

No. Rose sat up straight and clenched her hands. Aunt Alice had just given her the most exciting day of her life. How could that be wrong? She would *not* let Mother turn Aunt Alice out. She would argue and get Father's support and be as stubborn as a mule, so there!

The horse trotted in through the iron gates and Aunt Alice paid the driver. Rose glanced around. 'Maybe that wasn't her in the carriage.'

But as they walked up the steps, the front door swung open and there stood Mother, still wearing her hat and gloves. Her face was set like a stone mask, but her eyes glittered angrily.

'Where have you been, Rose?'

'Into town,' Rose said, wishing her stomach didn't have such huge butterflies bumping around in it. 'I ... we ... we saw Father.'

'Don't lie to me, Rose!' Mother stood back. 'Come inside. Now.'

Rose walked into the hallway, her legs shaking, her throat bone dry. She had never seen Mother so angry before, not even when Rose broke her favourite vase with her cricket ball.

'Alice, how dare you take my daughter into such a place!'

'Elizabeth, half of Melbourne has visited Coles Arcade,' Aunt Alice said calmly.

'Not the half I wish to be associated with,' Mother snapped. 'I want you to –'

Rose interrupted. 'Coles Arcade is a wonderful place, Mother, and Aunt Alice is not to blame. I asked to go there.'

Mother's face turned a deep red. 'That is a perfect example of what a bad influence you are, Alice. Whatever manners Rose might have had are nowhere to be seen. She has turned into the rudest child I have ever met!' Mother sucked in a deep breath, then spat out, 'Alice, you are no longer welcome under my roof.'

Rose was horrified. She opened her mouth to protest, but Aunt Alice said, 'Ah, but it's not your house, Elizabeth. I'll leave when Daniel asks me to, and not before.' She turned and walked up the stairs, her back straight, her head held high.

Mother stared down at Rose, her hands clasped so tightly in front of her that her knuckles were white. 'You are to go to your room and stay there until I say you may leave. That may be never. Go!'

Rose rushed up the stairs, tears spilling down her face, and slammed her door. Mother was the meanest, cruellest person in the whole world! How could she tell Aunt Alice to leave? It wasn't fair!

Rose paced around her room, muttering to

herself, then flung open her wardrobe doors. Lying on top of her underwear was the dreaded corset. That, she thought, is the cause of all of my troubles. And I intend to do something about it.

Rose pulled the corset out and dropped it on the floor. She stamped on it with both feet, but that wasn't enough. What else? She grabbed the scissors from her sewing basket and started cutting at the corset. Some parts were too stiff, but she made half a dozen satisfyingly large holes, then marched it out of her room and down the stairs.

Voices rang out from the drawing room. She stopped – Mother's voice was so loud, Rose could hear every word. Who was she talking to? Martha?

'It's not enough that she has ruined her own reputation, now she has to cast a shadow over our family, too!'

The bubbling anger inside Rose spilled over

like a red-hot fountain, and she pushed open the drawing-room door.

'Why are you being so unfair? Aunt Alice has done nothing – oh!' It wasn't Martha standing by the fireplace, it was Father.

'Rose, you seem a little upset.' Father's face was stern.

Rose's mouth took over before she could stop it. 'Mother is making me miserable! And she is angry with Aunt Alice for no good reason. It was you who told us to go to Parer's Crystal Palace for luncheon, Father, and it was wonderful, and so was Coles Arcade, which I have wanted to visit for ever so long, and Mother won't let me do anything interesting, and on top of all of that, she is trying to make me wear this!' With that, Rose threw the ruined corset on the floor.

Mother's face had gone from bright red to a strangely pale grey, and she sat down abruptly in an armchair. She fanned her face for a few moments and made little gasping noises. Rather than rush to her side, Father remained by the fireplace, looking at Rose with a bemused expression.

Finally, Mother managed to get some words out. 'The – the corset! Alice has turned our little girl into a . . . demon!' She suddenly looked up at Father. 'What does she mean – you told them to go to Parer's? They serve alcohol there! Surely Alice is not corrupting you, too?'

Rose knew in an instant that Mother had gone too far. The twinkle disappeared from Father's eyes and his moustache drew down at the corners. 'That is quite enough, Elizabeth. Alice is my sister, and she is welcome in this house for as long as she wishes to put up with your rudeness.'

'How could you?' Mother gasped again, and rose to her feet, taking a deep breath and thrusting out her chest. 'Very well, Daniel.

I will suffer her presence. But she must not be allowed to influence Rose.'

Rose knew what that meant – she wouldn't be allowed to spend any time with Aunt Alice at all. Rose planted her feet and put her hands on her hips. 'I will run away, then. If my life is to be nothing but stupid embroidery with Miss Parson and wearing something that squeezes me half to death, then I might as well run away.'

'Rose! How could you be so rude? Do you see *now* what I mean, Daniel?' Mother said. She was waving her fan about so much that Rose thought she might hit someone with it. 'What hope do we have that Rose will grow up and become a proper lady like Martha?'

Father looked down at the ruined corset, and then at Rose, who folded her arms tightly and stuck out her chin. She was not a young lady now and she never would be, so Mother had better get used to the idea. She met Father's gaze steadily, managing to hold back and wait for his answer.

He rubbed his chin slowly and nodded, as if having a conversation with himself. Rose's stomach began to do flips. Was he going to agree with Mother that she was rude and ill-behaved? She almost stopped breathing when he let out a heavy sigh. He couldn't let her down now – he couldn't!

'Elizabeth, I suspect that Rose will never be the kind of young lady you want her to be. Rose, what do you want to be when you grow up?' His tone was serious and Rose's knees felt wobbly.

'Married, of course,' Mother said. 'To someone from a suitable family.'

Rose shook her head. 'No, I don't. Today I thought I'd like to be a tram driver.' She ignored her mother's yelp of horror and went on. 'But I know I wouldn't be strong enough to pull on the grips. So instead I plan to go to university.'

'That's entirely possible now,' Father said. 'The University has been taking girls for a few years. What would you study?'

Rose wished she had a perfect answer, but decided she should just be honest.

'I don't know yet. There are so many things I am interested in – geology, history, how things are built, people from other lands.'

'Utterly ridiculous,' Mother said.

'You're not interested in business?' Father asked. 'You wouldn't want to take over the Emporium?'

Now Rose was sure she could see laughter in his eyes. 'No, thank you,' she said with a grin.

'You might think this is amusing, Daniel,' Mother said. 'But I will not have Rose bringing such disgrace on us. You forget what Melbourne society is like. What if she ruins Martha's chances of making a good match?'

Father sighed. 'Ah yes, Martha and Lord Elton's nephew. How could I forget?'

Rose bit her lip. Surely she wasn't spoiling things for Martha?

'Exactly,' Mother said. 'He's expected for dinner this evening, and instead of making sure the menu is ready, I have had to deal with Alice and Rose.'

'Then I will take over,' Father said. 'You must oversee this dinner as only you know how.' He shooed Mother out of the drawing room and turned back to Rose.

'So, it's university you have your heart set on, is it?'

'Yes, but Mother –'

'Your mother will be fine, now she has had her say. But . . .' He sat and took Rose's hands in his own large, warm ones. 'Rosie, I can see you are set on a different path, one that might cause you trouble and heartache. I suspect, though, that you are tough enough to stick it out. I'll do my best to help you, I promise.'

'Thank you, Father!' Rose thought for a

moment. 'But what about Martha? Am I really ruining her chances with Lord What's-His-Name?'

'I doubt it. Martha is not old enough for marriage yet, anyway.' He looked down at the shredded corset. 'And I agree – you are far too young to wear this. I will have it thrown out.'

Rose threw her arms around Father and hugged him tightly. 'Thank you. That's almost the best part of today – except for those monkeys in Coles Arcade.' She paused. 'May I ask for one more thing? Please?'

'Just one?' Father said, laughing.

Rose took a deep breath and screwed up all her courage. 'I'll never go to university if I have only Miss Parson to teach me. Father, I really, really want to go to school. Do you think it might be possible?'

'I'm sure it will be one day.' Father smiled, and tweaked her chin. 'The world is changing, and even your mother might find herself changing with it.'

And Rose had to be happy with that – for now.

HOW I BECAME AN AUSTRALIAN GIRL

by Sheryl Clark

I was born and grew up in New Zealand, on a dairy farm, and travelled all the way around the world before I eventually came to Australia. My oldest sister, Karen, was a world traveller and I wanted to be just like her.

I arrived in Australia in 1978. I was only planning to stay for three months but I'm still here, and now I am a citizen.

At school, I learned a lot about European history but nothing about Australia. I had no idea how the government worked, or that the states were independent until Federation. And what was Federation anyway?

Writing Rose's story meant a huge amount of research, which I love, and I suspect I now know more about early Melbourne and Federation than most Aussies!

HOW I BECAME AN AUSTRALIAN GIRL

by *Lucia Masciullo*

I was born and grew up in Italy, a beautiful country to visit, but also a difficult country to live in for new generations.

In 2006, I packed up my suitcase and I left Italy with the man I love. We bet on Australia. I didn't know much about Australia before coming – I was just looking for new opportunities, I guess.

And I liked it right from the beginning! Australian people are resourceful, open-minded and always with a smile on their faces. I think all Australians keep in their blood a bit of the pioneer heritage, regardless of their own birthplace.

Here I began a new life and now I'm doing what I always dreamed of: I illustrate stories. Here is the place where I'd like to live and to grow up my children, in a country that doesn't fear the future.

In 1900, life was a lot more restrictive for women than it is today. In most parts of Australia, women weren't allowed to vote. Only a few got the chance to go to university, and it was difficult for women to have careers of their own.

This conservatism was reflected in the clothing of the time. Women wore floor-length dresses with large puffed sleeves and high necklines. Corsets that shaped you into the letter S were very popular, and girls as young as six might wear one. If you were going out, you always wore a hat and gloves, and on sunny days a parasol to shade you from the sun was a must.

Girls wore smock dresses and pinafores until they were fourteen or so. The fashion was to wear white, so you can imagine how hard that would have been to keep clean.

Most women had long hair that they curled in rags or papers. If your hair was thin, you could put a horsehair pad on your head and pin your hair over it to make it look thicker.

Well-to-do women had their clothing made by tailors. The first ready-made clothes were blouses, and were usually worn by poorer women. Some women wore pantaloons, so they could ride bicycles and play sport, but these were frowned upon as being unladylike.

Girls like Rose and women like Aunt Alice had to fight for the rights they felt entitled to. They were modern thinkers, ahead of their time, and made it possible for Australian girls today to have many choices – not only in the clothes they wear but in the lives they lead.

The Suffragettes

The suffragettes often used posters to help their campaigns. Strong images could really get their message across, especially to those who couldn't read well.

DID YOU KNOW THAT IN 1900 . . .

There was a fire in the roof of
Buckingham Palace.

Women in Germany demanded to be allowed
to go to university.

Over 1,000 tonnes of waste was removed from
demolished buildings in Sydney after an
outbreak of the bubonic plague.

In France, the length of a legal workday
for women and children was limited to
11 hours.

Hawaii became part of the United States.

The King of Italy was assassinated.

There was a hurricane in Texas.

The Olympic Games were held in Paris.

Coca-Cola went on sale in Britain for
the first time.

A group of schoolgirls disappeared at
Hanging Rock.

Want to find out more?

Turn the page for a
sneak peek at Book 2

Rose on Wheels

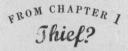

FROM CHAPTER 1
Thief?

ROSE ran along the hallway to Aunt Alice's room, tapped on the door and rushed in, banging the door back against the wall. 'Aunt Alice, do you think – oh!' She stopped short. The person who stood in front of her was not Aunt Alice.

It was Miss Parson! The governess froze, colour leeching from her face, her mouth open. She clutched something tightly in one hand.

Rose's heart banged against her ribs. 'Are

you . . . are you supposed to be in here?'

'I . . . I came to . . . borrow a book,' Miss Parson stuttered.

Rose stared at Miss Parson – she wasn't holding any books at all, but her hand was still clenched. 'What have you got there?'

'Nothing. Er . . . one of my hair pins fell out, that's all.' Miss Parson took a shuddering breath and moved forward, brushing past Rose and heading for the hallway without another word.

Phew! Rose was baffled, but she had a feeling Miss Parson had been lying. Rose checked Aunt Alice's drawers and, sure enough, it looked like someone had been rummaging through them. She opened the jewellery box but she couldn't tell if anything was missing. She'd have to ask Aunt Alice later.

Rose's heartbeat slowly returned to

normal while she puzzled over Miss Parson's behaviour. Was she just snooping? She'd often snooped in Rose's room. And if she was stealing things, why? Was she so very poor, like the people Rose had seen being evicted from their house in town? Yet she had a room in Rose's house to live in, plenty of food to eat, and a yearly wage. Maybe she had debts? thought Rose. But if so, why didn't she steal really valuable things that she could sell?

These worrying thoughts were like sharp teeth nibbling at her. Aunt Alice mightn't be back for ages, and there was no use asking Mother – she'd demand an explanation and then Miss Parson would be in tremendous trouble. Mother would dismiss her, and maybe she'd even go to gaol. That would be awful! Even if she was stealing, Rose didn't want bad things to happen to her.

Father was at the Emporium. Edward was at school. What about Martha? Rose walked to the other end of the hallway, to Martha's room, and knocked.

'Who is it?' Martha called in a soft voice.

'Rose.'

'Come in,' Martha said.

Rose entered and found Martha's room in near-darkness. The curtains were closed and no lights were on, apart from a small lamp on the wall. Martha lay on her bed, a cloth over her eyes. Thoughts of Miss Parson flew out of Rose's head. 'Are you sick?' she asked anxiously.

'Just a headache,' Martha whispered. 'It'll go away soon.'

'Oh. I'll go away too, then.'

'No, no, stay,' Martha said. 'I hardly ever see you anymore, or talk to you.'

'Well, you're very busy dressing up with Mother and thinking about getting married,' Rose said. She plopped herself down on the chair next to Martha's bed and leant forward, resting her arms on the bedcovers. 'Maybe that's why you have a headache. Your brain is tired of hats and hair and hat pins.'

Martha smiled. 'I think my head is tired of Lord Elton's nephew, Raymond.'

'Is he handsome?' Rose asked. 'Or is he rich?'

'He's both,' Martha said, 'but he is a complete ninny. Spends all his time gambling and riding horses and pretending he is someone special. Ugh!' She shuddered. 'I'd rather die than marry someone like that.'

'Me, too.' Rose stroked Martha's forehead, and sprinkled cool water from a jug onto the cloth.

'Oh that is so nice,' Martha said. 'Anyway, Raymond says he may go back to England next week, thank goodness.' She closed her eyes and Rose waited, and then wondered if she had fallen asleep.

But a smile crept across Martha's face. 'I still can't believe you cut up your corset.'

'Mother nearly had a fit!' The memory still made Rose laugh, even though it was weeks ago.

'Good for you. The corset she bought me is hurting my back terribly, but she won't listen. I may have to take to it with the scissors.' She opened her eyes and stared at Rose. 'Now, something is bothering you, I can tell, and it's not the corset. What is it?'

Rose hesitated. Could she really accuse Miss Parson without knowing for sure if she'd taken something?

Rose McCubbin . 1900.

Meet the other Australian girls and authors

MEET GRACE
1808

It's 1808 and Grace is living with her uncle in London. They have no money, and Grace is always lonely and often hungry. One afternoon, Grace can't resist taking a shiny red apple from a grocer's cart – and then another...Before she knows it, Grace is being chased through the streets! Will she be caught and sent to prison – or worse?

Meet Grace and join her adventure in the first of four exciting stories about a convict girl who is given a second chance.

Sofie Laguna, author of the Grace books, is a highly regarded and award-winning writer of books for children. *Bird and Sugar Boy* was an Honour Book in the 2007 CBCA Book of the Year Awards, Younger Readers, and Sofie's adult book, *One Foot Wrong*, was longlisted for the Miles Franklin Award in 2009.

MEET LETTY
1841

It's 1841 and Letty is on the docks in England, farewelling her bossy older sister who is about to take a long sea voyage to Australia. But then there's a mix-up, and before she knows it Letty finds herself on the ship too, travelling to New South Wales! How will Letty manage when her sister doesn't even want her on the ship? And what will it be like on the other side of the world?

Meet Letty and join her adventure in the first of four exciting stories about a free-settler girl and her new life in a far-off land.

Alison Lloyd, author of the Letty books, is the popular and highly regarded author of several books for children, including *Year of the Tiger* and *Wicked Warriors and Evil Emperors*, a fantastic and fact-filled book about Ancient China.

Meet Poppy
1864

It's 1864 and Poppy lives at Bird Creek Mission near Echuca. Poppy hates the Mission, especially now that her brother, Gus, has run away to pan for gold. What if Poppy escaped, too? Would she survive alone in the bush? And would she ever find Gus, whom she loves more than anything in the world?

Meet Poppy and join her adventure in the first of four stories about a Gold Rush girl who dreams of a better life.

Gabrielle Wang, author of the Poppy books, is a much loved writer for young people. Gabrielle's recent books include her bestselling Young Adult novel *Little Paradise,* and the very popular *Ghost in My Suitcase* which won the 2009 Aurealis Award for young fiction.

OUR
AUSTRALIAN
GIRL

ouraustraliangirl.com.au

Want to find out more?
For all the latest news, behind-the-scenes
information and to enter competitions,
visit our website. We'd love to hear from you!

Follow the story of your favourite
Australian girls and you will see that there
is a special charm on the cover of each book
that tells you something about the story.

Here they all are. You can tick them
off as you read each one.

Meet Grace

A Friend
for Grace

Grace
and Glory

A Home
for Grace

MEET LETTY

LETTY AND THE
STRANGER'S LACE

LETTY
ON THE LAND

LETTY'S
CHRISTMAS

Meet Poppy

Poppy at
Summerhill

Poppy and
the Thief

Poppy
Comes Home

Meet Rose

Rose on Wheels

Rose's
Challenge

Rose in Bloom

A girl like me in a time gone by